Uncle Amon

FINLEY THE FISH

Stories, Jokes, Games, and More!

Table of Contents

Finley the Fish

Finley the Fish is an adorable little fish that likes to swim with his friend, Barney, each day. There are other fish that Finley swims with but lately Finley has found that the other fish seem to want to be alone.

"I just don't understand it," said Finley. "Do they not like me anymore?"

Finley's best friend, Barney, just swam past him. Barney is a big brown fish. He has been friends with Finley for a very long time and Finley always seeks advice from him. Finley trusts Barney's advice. Barney has never steered him wrong.

"Who doesn't like you anymore?" asked Barney.

"My other fish friends that I sometimes swim with," said Finley. "It seems that lately they just want to be alone."

"You know," said Barney. "There is actually nothing wrong with wanting to be alone from time to time."

"You think so," said Finley. "I don't like to be alone. I love having my friends to swim with me."

"I like to be alone sometimes," said Barney.

"You do?" asked Finley.

"Yes," said Barney. "I do."

"Why?" asked Finley. "Why would you want to be alone?"

"Well," said Barney. "I like to be alone so I can gather my thoughts and think about things."

"Hmmm," said Finley. "I do like to think about things."

"When you think about things," said Barney. "Do you ever notice that when you are with someone, they sometimes interrupt your thoughts and then a lot of times you can't remember what it was you were thinking about?"

"Actually," said Finley. "Yes, that has happened to me."

"This is just a suggestion," said Barney. "But maybe you need some time for yourself."

"You think so," said Finley, thinking about what Barney had just said.

"It might help you to sort through your thoughts," said Barney. "It might help you to think better as well. Why don't you try it?"

"I guess it wouldn't hurt to try," said Finley.

That afternoon Finley decided that he would go spend some time by himself. He headed out into the deep waters and started to look around.

"It is nice out here," said Finley. "It sure is quiet though, maybe a little too quiet."

Finley wasn't sure if he liked the idea of being alone. He kept expecting to hear Barney's voice or one of the other fish. However, it didn't take Finley long to start enjoying the peace and quiet of the open water. He found that he could do some serious thinking without anyone bothering him.

"I was wondering if you wanted to swim with me today?" asked Barney.

"No," said Finley. "I have some more thinking to do."

The next day, Barney asked Finley to hang out with him again and Finley said no to him once more.

"Okay," said Barney the next day. "I think you are spending too much time alone."

"I am really enjoying my time alone though," said Finley. "I can actually think without being bothered by someone."

"Yes," said Barney. "I know it is nice to spend some time alone. However, you have to spend time with your friends too."

Finley thought about what Barney said and he knew he was right. Finley started spending his morning with his friends and his afternoons by himself. That way he was able to see his friends and still have time for himself.

Finley's Best Friend, Barney

Finley the Fish was swimming in the water beside his best friend, Barney.

"It sure is a nice day to be swimming," said Finley.

"Yes," said Barney, looking up toward the top of the water. "It looks like the sun is shining bright."

"I love when the sun is shining," said Finley. "I like how the sunlight leaves rays of light through the water."

"Yes," said Barney. "The colors the sun turns the water makes it very beautiful."

Finley looked at Barney and he knew Barney had something on his mind. Barney looked pre-occupied.

"Do you have something you want to ask me?" asked Finley. "You seem like you are pre-occupied."

"Well," said Barney. "There is a race I wanted to enter. I wondered if you would like to enter it as well."

"I don't know," said Finley. "I don't think we are very fit to be entering such a race."

"We can train for it," said Barney. "We have about a week."

"Do you think that is enough time?" asked Finley.

"If we work really hard at it," said Barney. "We can be ready in a week."

"Okay," said Finley. "I will enter the race with you."

Finley and Barney trained really hard over the next few days. They put all their effort into it. In fact, they trained so hard that Finley did end up injuring his tail.

"Oh dear!" exclaimed Finley at the end of training that day. "My tail is so sore. How am I ever going to be able to enter the race?"

"Well," said Barney. "We will just have to hope that you heal fast otherwise we will have to cancel."

"I don't want to cancel," said Finley, who was very determined to win the race.

The next day, Finley was out swimming around, waiting for Barney to show up to train.

"What took you so long?" asked Finley when Barney showed up.

"Well," said Barney. "I didn't think you were going to make it to training today because of your tail."

"My tail is actually starting to feel better," said Finley. "Moving around is helping me get over the pain."

"Okay good," said Barney. "Let's get this training started."

Finley did put a good effort into training and by the end of the day his tail was pretty sore but he was still determined to win the race.

"Good luck," said Barney on the day of the race. "Let's see if we can win it."

Finley and Barney swam as quickly as they could and Barney was very surprised to see that Finley was actually at the finish line ahead of everyone else including him.

"I am so proud of you!" exclaimed Barney, catching up to Finley. "How is your tail?"

"I think it is actually much better," said Finley.

"There is a race next weekend too," said Barney. "Do you want to enter it?"

"Yes," said Finley. "That would be great!"

George the Green Fish

Finley the Fish was swimming with his best friend, Barney. Finley saw a big green fish swim by and he was mesmerized by it.

"Did you just see that green fish swim by?" asked Finley.

"Yes," said Barney. "I did. He had the coolest green scales I've ever seen!"

"He sure did," said Finley. "I would like to be his friend."

"Yes," said Barney. "I think that would be a good idea."

"How will we get him to be our friend?" asked Finley.

"We will need to find him and ask him," said Barney.

"I am too afraid to talk to him," said Finley, feeling shy all of a sudden.

"There is nothing to be shy about," said Barney. "You just go up to him and say hello and start talking to him."

"Do you really think it will be that easy?" asked Finley.

"Oh yes," said Barney, confidently. "Do you remember how we met?"

"Yes," said Finley, thinking back to the day he first saw Barney swimming in the water. "I do remember."

"What was the very first thing you said to me?" asked Barney.

"I think I said hello and then I asked you if you wanted to be my friend," said Finley.

"Yes," said Barney. "That is correct. Did you really find it hard to talk to me?"

"I guess not," said Finley. "Once I got talking to you, I found it very easy."

"Okay," said Barney. "Let's go find the green fish and see if he will be our friend."

Finley and Barney swam in the direction they saw the green fish swimming. It took them about a half an hour but they did finally find him. The green fish was eating some plants in a cavern.

"Hello," said the green fish, noticing Finley and Barney entering the cavern.

"Hi," said Finley, who was very relieved that he didn't have to be the one to start the conversation.

"My name is George," said the green fish.

"This is my friend Barney," said Finley. "I am Finley."

Finley and Barney swam with George for the rest of the afternoon. They found George was a very caring fish and the three immediately became good friends.

"Please come back and swim with me tomorrow," said George, when it was starting to get dark outside.

"Yes," said Finley and Barney together. "We would like to do that."

The three friends had a lot of fun swimming around together. Finley and Barney both found that when there were big fish were swimming around them, George would help protect them.

"Thank you George," said Finley, after George had scared away some bigger fish that were bothering him and Barney.

"That is what friends are for," said George.

Finley Meets a Shark

Finley the Fish was sound asleep in the waters near the entrance to his friend, Barney's home. He was in a very deep sleep and he started to have a dream that he was being chased by a shark. Finley woke up and he was a little scared after that dream.

"Finley," said Barney, seeing that Finlay had just woken up. "Are you okay?"

"I just had a terrible dream," said Finley. "I dreamt that I was being chased by a shark."

"Oh dear," said Barney. "I will tell you what. If I see a shark, I will tell it to stay out of your dreams for you."

"Oh," said Finley. "That would be wonderful."

Finley was very grateful that he had a caring friend such as Barney. Barney always knew the right thing to do and he always knew the right thing to say.

"You just leave it up to me," said Barney. "You will not see any more sharks in your dreams."

Finley was confident that Barney would do as he said so the next day, he saw a shark swimming pretty close to him and he went right up to the shark and talked to him.

"Mr. Shark," said Finley. "My friend Barney told me he was going to talk to you and tell you to stay out of my dreams."

"I don't know who this Barney is," said the shark. "He never talked to me. However, if you want me to stay out of your dreams, I will do so."

"You will," said Finley, suddenly feeling even smaller than his actual size against the massive size of the shark. "I would greatly appreciate that."

Finley talked to Barney later that day and Barney apologized to Finley telling him that he didn't have time to talk to the shark yet.

"I know," said Finley, telling Barney all about his encounter with the shark.

"You actually told the shark yourself to stay out of your dreams," said Barney, amazed at Finley's new found confidence.

"I did," said Finley.

"Oh Finley," said Barney. "I am so proud of you!"

"Thank you," said Finley, feeling very good about himself.

The next time Finley and Barney were playing, they came across an octopus.

"I am afraid of an octopus," said Barney.

"You are!" exclaimed Finley.

"Yes," said Barney.

"Well," said Finley, remembering how he had found the confidence to stand up to the shark the other day. "The best way to get over your fears is to face them."

"I suppose you are right," said Barney.

Barney went right up to the octopus and talked to him.

"I was afraid of you," said Barney. "I am not afraid now though."

"Good," said the octopus. "I am not a creature that you need to be afraid of at all."

Finley was very proud of Barney for facing his fears.

"I guess we have both learned to face our fears," said Finley.

"Yes," said Barney. "We sure did!"

Finley Meets the Colorful Fish

Finley was swimming in the deep waters one cool autumn day. The waters were actually very cold.

"You know," said Barney, Finley's best friend. "This is the time of the year that the most colorful fish start swimming around these parts of the water."

"Oh yes," said Finley. "I remember those colorful fish from last year. They were very beautiful with all their glorious colors."

"They sure were," said Barney. "I am looking forward to seeing them again."

"Do you think they will let us swim with them?" asked Finley. "They did last year. We had so much fun with them."

"I am not sure," said Barney. "Are you going to be scared of them this year like you were last year?"

"No," said Finley, thinking before he answered Barney's question. "I don't think I will be scared of them this year."

"I am not sure why you were so scared of them last year," said Barney.

"I think it was because their colors were so bright and vibrant," said Finley. "Also, I wasn't expecting them to be there."

"Yes," said Barney. "I do suppose that is true."

Finley and Barney looked around every stone and cavern on the bottom of the water for the colorful fish. It was a few days before they actually seen them.

"Oh my!" exclaimed Finley, holding his breath when he did see one. "Look! It is the colorful fish!"

"It is!" exclaimed Barney.

Both Finley and Barney were mesmerized by the colors in the fish that they saw. There were bright greens, blues, and the most gleaming yellow color they had ever seen.

"How would you like to swim with us again this year?" one of the colorful fish asked Finley and Barney.

"We would love to!" exclaimed Finley.

"We are honored that you remembered us," said Barney.

"Of course we remembered you," said one of the colorful fish. "We were such good friends last year. It was fun swimming with you."

"We thought so too," said Finley.

Finley and Barney swam with the colorful fish and they were so proud too!

"I think I want to invite the colorful fish to my birthday party tomorrow," said Finley.

"Oh yes," said Barney. "I think they would like that."

The colorful fish came to Finley's birthday party and everyone had so much fun. Finley's other friends were mesmerized by the beautiful colors of the colorful fish. Once they became accustomed to their bright colors, they became good friends with the colorful fish too.

"We must go away again," said the colorful fish a few days later. "We would like everyone to swim with us one more time before we go."

Every fish in the lake that Finley and Barney lived swam with the colorful on their last swim before they had to swim away.

"We will watch for you next year at this time," said Finley, waving to the colorful fish.

"We look forward to it," said the colorful fish.

Finley, Barney and all the other fish were sad to see the colorful fish leave but they were happy that they would see them again next year. They were looking forward to their next visit.

Just for Fun Activity

Finley the Fish met some nice friends in the above stories. Please write a paragraph or more about how you met your best friend.

Funny Jokes for Kids

Q: Why are fish so smart?

A: They are always in a school!

Q: What is a knight's favorite fish?

A: Swordfish!

Q: What fish makes the best sandwiches?

A: The peanut butter and jellyfish!

Q: Why are fish bad at tennis?

A: They don't like to get close to the net!

Q: What fish is best to have in a boat?

A: A sailfish!

Q: Why is a fish easy to weigh?

A: It has its own scales!

Q: How do the fish get to school?

A: On an octobus!

Q: Where do fish go to borrow money?

A: A loan shark!

Q: Which fish only swims at night?

A: Starfish!

Q: How do you communicate with a fish?

A: Drop it a line!

HOW MANY FISH DO YOU SEE?

Can you find your way through the maze?

Can you find your way through the maze?

Can you find your way through the maze?

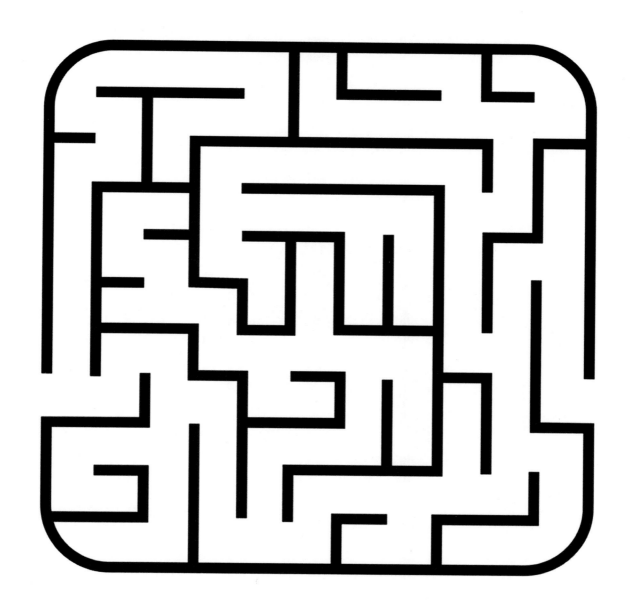

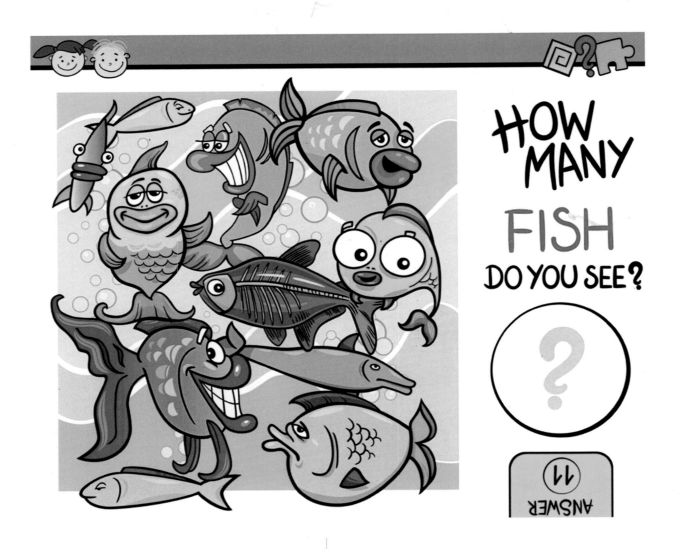

HOW MANY FISH DO YOU SEE?

?

ANSWER 11